3-D CHILLERS

VAMPIRES, ZOMBIES, AND WEREWOLVES

Your 3-D adventure starts here. When you see this symbol, slip on the 3-D glasses and watch as the terrifying creatures jump out at you!

SCHOLASTIC

New York • Toronto • London • Auckland
Sydney • Mexico City • New Delhi • Hong Kong

NIGHT FEEDER

It's a good idea to be prepared for a zombie attack at all times, but you should be especially alert at night. This is when zombies stagger out of their hiding places. Expert night hunters, zombies rely on their sharp senses of smell and hearing to track down their victims.

CHILLING FACT

Modern zombies have only one aim—to devour people's flesh. That is why they are so determined to follow you around and break into your home!

TOXIC HORROR

Modern zombies are diseased creatures who multiply and spread like the plague. Whichever way you turn, they are likely to appear. These toxic beasts with their rotting brains show no emotion or reason. They just groan and moan as they sink their teeth into your tasty flesh!

DEADLY OUTBREAK

How modern zombies came about is a mystery. They may be people who fell victim to an unknown disease or were infected by an airborne virus, or perhaps a poisonous chemical leaked into their bodies. One thing is certain, however: If you find one zombie, there will be more. A zombie outbreak will spread far and wide!

WHO IS TO BLAME?

Until moviemaker George A. Romero started making zombie movies in the 1960s, the modern zombie didn't exist. Romero created ghoulish monsters who infected the world and caused society to break down. This plague of the undead was known as the zombie apocalypse. The movies were extremely popular and some have recently been remade.

DO I SMELL?

You can spot a modern zombie a mile away. It will have rotting flesh and bulging eyes, and bits of its body will probably be dropping off. It will also most definitely stink! On no account try to fight this hideous creature. It will feel no pain even if you injure it, so you can never win.

ZOMBIE ATTACK!

Once a zombie attack occurs, it is important to equip yourself with the skills to survive. Remember, if you get bitten or come into contact with infected flesh, you too will become a zombie. Don't trust people with cuts or blood on their body. Once you have been infected, the countdown to your reanimation may be only a few hours.

OFF WITH ITS HEAD!

If you're feeling brave, you can try killing a zombie. Don't bother with stakes through the heart. The only way to finish off this creature is to destroy its brain. If you have an ax on hand, a clean option is to chop off its head. Another effective method is to use a blunt instrument such as a baseball bat to bash it over the head. But remember, the zombie skull is hard!

GET OUT OF HERE!

When dealing with zombies, your first line of defense is to find a safe place to hide. Barricade yourself indoors. Zombies aren't good at breaking in, but they will freak you out by hammering on the windows, so try to stay calm. Another tactic is to shuffle along and pretend you're a zombie, too. But this tactic will probably only work for a short time!

ZOMBIE SURVIVAL KIT

This kit may mean the difference between life and death! Keep it under your bed at all times. You never know when you may need it!

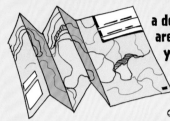

a detailed map of the area—to help you find your way around

a mask—to protect you from infection

a flashlight and batteries—in case electricity supplies are cut

bottles of water, cans of food, and a can opener—for long days in hiding

padded waterproof clothing—for surviving outdoors

PLANET TERROR

The worst-case scenario is Z-day—when zombies take over the planet. If this happens, humans will be living in isolated groups and often on the move. You'll need to use all your survival skills. Start training now to get as fit as possible. Pack your survival kit and practice building campfires on which to burn infected bodies.

ZOMBIE APOCALYPSE

The idea of a zombie apocalypse, when the diseased walking dead could soon be the last creatures on Earth, has taken the world by storm. There has been much discussion about this chilling topic, especially of how the few remaining uninfected people would need to battle to survive to save the human race.

LAST PERSON ALIVE

Imagine you were the last healthy human alive, and flesh-hunting zombies were after you! You would need a well-protected house. During the day, you could go out for supplies, but be careful—some zombies feed in the daytime, too. At night, all doors and windows would need to be bolted and barred against the attackers.

ESCAPING THE CROWD

One survival tactic is to try to make your escape from the diseased, moaning crowds who are following you around. It may help if you locate a group of survivors. Then you can all work together to distract the mindless creatures. This will give you the chance to get out of town and find a zombie-free zone.

NOT CLOWNING AROUND

Another good idea is to set yourself some zombie survival rules, such as checking the backseat of your car for zombies and not entering a tiny bathroom with only one exit! A sense of humor is also useful during these grim times. Who knows what kind of zombie you might meet?!

MUMMIES, SLAVES, AND SKELETONS

Zombies have a long history—descriptions of the walking dead date back to ancient times. The first true zombies were the slavelike creatures who form part of the folklore of West Africa and the Caribbean, in particular the island of Haiti. These are the voodoo zombies.

VOODOO TERROR

MINDLESS MUMMY

Ancient Egyptian mummies are not technically zombies. However, their bandaged bodies remain preserved for thousands of years, so they can easily come back to life! Legend tells us that if you open a mummy's tomb, the creature will wake up and punish you with a terrible curse!

Voodoo zombies look like sickly humans and have no will of their own. They are created by a powerful sorcerer, called a *bokor*, who controls their actions. Legend says that a *bokor* can raise the dead through rituals, spells, and potions. He captures the dead person's soul, turning the victim into a zombie slave. The *bokor* then puts the soul in a jar and uses it to strengthen his own power.

SKELETON WARRIOR

As long ago as the third century BC, the ancient Greeks feared the undead! In the story of Jason and the Argonauts, the mythological hero, Jason, battles with an army of creepy skeletons who have risen from the ground. Jason must defeat the skeleton zombies in his quest to become king.

CHILLING FACT
The word *zombie* comes from the African word *nzambi*, which means "soul of a dead person."

27

BACK FROM THE GRAVE

Around the world, you will find many stories about zombielike creatures, including Nordic *draugrs* and Arabian ghouls. While these walking dead may not strictly be classified as zombies, they share many of their features. It's time to meet the zombies' spooky cousins!

SUPERHUMAN CORPSE

In Norse legend, the *draugr* was a dead Viking who had come back to life. The creature left its grave at night, roamed the countryside, and attacked everything in its path. The *draugr* possessed superhuman strength and could make its body swell up to an enormous size.

WERE-BEASTS ROUND THE WORLD

Check out this world tour of other legendary shape-shifting creatures.

Giant were-cats resembling fierce cougars are rumored to prowl the rocky slopes of North America.

In Iceland, frightening *hamrammr* can transform into whatever animal they have just eaten.

ICELAND

NORTH AMERICA

JAPAN

The *chonchon* of Chile appear as feathered birds with freakish human heads. Their ears form hideous, gigantic wings.

CHILE

Kitsune are cunning Japanese witches. They usually appear as foxes but can shape-shift into human form.

43

WEREWOLF MOVIE MANIA

Today, most people aren't frightened of werewolves waiting to pounce on them around every corner. Even so, we can still scare ourselves silly at the movies. From black-and-white classics to recent monster blockbusters, these fang-toothed films are guaranteed to send chills down our spines!

CREEPY CLASSICS

One of the earliest Hollywood werewolf movies was *The Wolf Man* (1941). In it, actor Lon Chaney Jr. sprouted fur and claws after being bitten by a werewolf and was eventually killed by his father. *The Wolf Man* was a huge hit and encouraged the idea that werewolves could be slain with silver weapons.

MONSTER MAD

In the 1950s and 1960s, horror films went monster mad, but werewolves did not feature much. One exception was *The Curse of the Werewolf* (1961). In this low-budget B movie, made by Hammer Films in England, a woman rescued from the forest gives birth to a boy on Christmas Day. The movie draws on the belief that you are more likely to become a werewolf if you are born on Christmas!

Since the 1980s, werewolf movies have made a huge comeback. From *An American Werewolf in London* (1981), to *Underworld* (2003) and a remake of *The Wolfman* (2010), slasher-clawed movies are box-office dynamite. Even the Harry Potter movies feature a wizard werewolf in the shape of Professor Remus Lupin.

WOLF HERO

In recent years, the werewolf myth has been turned on its head. Today there are even werewolf heroes! Jacob Black, from the Twilight movie series, is the leader of a pack of Native American werewolves who shape-shift at will. In the X-Men films, Wolverine is a superhero with steel claws, keen senses, and the ability to heal from wounds instantly. It looks as though this new breed of wolfman is here to stay!

DICTIONARY OF THE SUPERNATURAL

Asanbosam
An imaginary creature from Africa with iron teeth. It lives in the trees and drains people of their blood.

Beast of Gévaudan
A wolflike creature rumored to have attacked people in France between 1764 and 1767.

Bokor
A powerful sorcerer who creates and controls a voodoo zombie.

Count Dracula
The most famous vampire. Dracula is a fictional character created by the novelist Bram Stoker.

Draugr
A dead Viking who has come back to life. A *draugr* possesses immense strength and supernatural powers.

Fangs
Long, pointed teeth for piercing flesh. Vampires and werewolves usually have fangs.

Ghoul
An evil spirit, usually found in graveyards, that feasts on human flesh.

Jiang shi
A Chinese ghost. It hops around and kills people by draining them of their energy.

Loup-garou
The French name for a werewolf, used in parts of Canada. *Loup* means "wolf" in French.

Lycanthrope
Another name for a werewolf.

Manananggal
A mythical flying female creature from the Philippines. It can split its body into two halves to hunt for human flesh.

Mummy
The preserved, bandaged body of an ancient Egyptian. Mummies are rumored to come back to life.

Mythology
A collection of ancient stories from a particular time or place, such as ancient Greece. They are usually about gods, magic, or supernatural beings.

Nagual
A Mexican witch that has the power to turn itself into a dog or other animal, such as a donkey.

Outbreak
A sudden increase in number, such as a growing group of zombies or a spreading disease.

Plague

An outbreak of a disease over a wide area. When there is a plague, people are infected rapidly.

Reanimate

To come back to life.

Revenant

A corpse that has returned from the dead to terrorize the living. Vampires, zombies, ghosts, and ghouls are all revenants.

Shape-shifter

A person who changes into another form, such as from a man to a wolf. Often a shape-shifter can transform at will.

Toxic

Highly poisonous.

Vampire

A person who has come back from the dead to drink the blood of the living.

Vampirisim

The practice of being a vampire.

Voodoo zombie

A corpse that has come back to life and is under the control of a powerful master.

Werewolf

A human who changes into a hairy, wolflike creature on the night of a full moon. A werewolf cannot control this transformation.

Wolfsbane

A poisonous plant that was used in the Middle Ages to attempt to cure werewolves.

Z-day

The day when zombies take over the planet and there are more zombies than humans.

Zombie

A diseased corpse with no reason or feeling that has come back to life to eat human flesh.

Zombie apocalypse

The name given to the breakdown of society after zombies have taken over the earth.

Zombie walk

A planned walk where people dress up and pretend to be zombies.

This edition created in 2011 by
Arcturus Publishing Limited, 26/27 Bickels Yard,
151-153 Bermondsey Street,
London SE1 3HA

ISBN 978-0-545-38779-8

10 9 8 7 6 5 4 3 2 1   11 12 13 14 15

Printed in Malaysia 106

First Scholastic edition, September 2011

ARCTURUS CREDITS:
Author: Deborah Kespert
Editor: Kate Overy
Design: Picnic
Illustrations: Flameboy, The Comic Stripper

PHOTO CREDITS:
Alamy: title page right; p. 5; p. 8; pp. 8-9; p. 14 bottom; p. 17
bottom; p. 19 top; p. 23 bottom; p. 29 top; p. 30; p. 35; p. 36
top; p. 37; p. 39 top and bottom; p. 41 top

Corbis: p. 12 right; p. 14 top; p. 31 top; p. 34; p. 42

Getty Images: p. 12 left

Kobal Collection: front cover left and right; title page left and
center; p. 4; p. 6 center and bottom; p. 7; p. 9 top; p. 10; p. 13;
p. 16 top and bottom; p. 17 top; pp. 18-19; p. 20 center and
bottom; p. 21; p. 22; p. 23 top; p. 24; pp. 24-25; p. 25 bottom;
p. 26; p. 27; p. 29 bottom; pp. 30-31; p. 32; p. 33; p. 36 bottom;
p. 44 top and bottom; p. 45 top and bottom

Rex Features: p. 11

Science Photo Library: p. 41 center

3-D images produced by Pinsharp